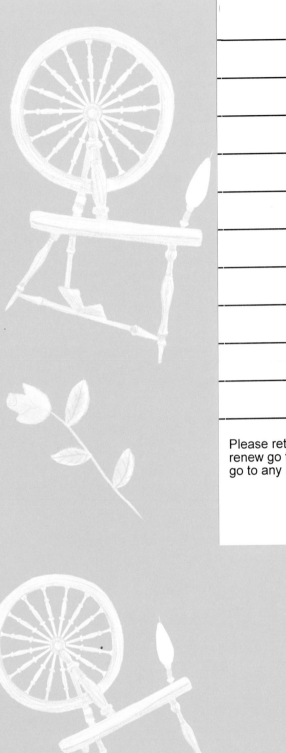

This book belongs to:

....

....

Quarto is the authority on a wide range of topics.

Quarto educates, entertains and enriches the lives of our readers—enthusiasts and lovers of hands-on living.

www.quartoknows.com

Author: Amanda Askew
Illustrator: Ayesha L. Rubio
Designer: Victoria Kimonidou
Editor: Ellie Brough

First Published in 2018 by QED Publishing,
an imprint of The Quarto Group.
The Old Brewery, 6 Blundell Street,
London N7 9BH, United Kingdom.
T (0)20 7700 6700 F (0)20 7700 8066
www.QuartoKnows.com

A catalogue record for this book is available from the British Library.

ISBN 978 1 78493 214 5

Manufactured in Dongguan, China TL112017

9 8 7 6 5 4 3 2 1

Sleeping Beauty

Written by Amanda Askew
Illustrated by Ayesha L. Rubio

Long ago, there lived a king and queen who
gave birth to a beautiful baby girl, named Rose.

The king could not contain his joy. He held a great feast to celebrate.
He invited friends, family and twelve fairies who lived in his kingdom.

After an amazing feast, each of the fairies gave Rose a magical gift.

The first fairy gave her the gift of kindness,

the second gave her the gift of beauty...

...and the third, the gift of intelligence.

As the twelfth fairy was about to give her gift, the party was interrupted by the arrival of a thirteenth fairy.

The thirteenth fairy was angry that she had not been invited. Everyone had forgotten her because she had not left her tower in years.

She cursed the child, "When the princess is fifteen years old, she will prick her finger with a spindle and fall down dead!"

The king and queen fell to the floor, sobbing.

The twelfth fairy, whose gift had not been given, stepped forward. "Fear not, Rose shall not die. Instead she will fall into a deep sleep lasting one hundred years and will be woken by a true love's kiss."

Over the years, the promises of the fairies came true.

Rose grew to be kind...

...beautiful...

...and clever.

The king and queen ordered every spindle across the kingdom
to be destroyed and they never told Rose of the curse.

On the morning of her fifteenth birthday, Rose woke early. She wandered through the halls and gardens until she felt curiously drawn in one direction.

She came to an old tower that she had never seen before.

Rose climbed the winding staircase
and opened a little door.

In a small room sat an old woman
with a spindle, busily spinning wool.

"What are you doing?"
asked the princess.

"I'm spinning. Would you like
to try?" asked the old woman.

The princess had hardly begun when she pricked her finger. At that moment, she fell into a deep sleep. The old woman was in fact the thirteenth fairy.

The king and queen burst into the room, but it was too late.

The king and queen laid their daughter in a
beautiful chamber at the top of the castle.

Not wanting to live without her, they asked
the twelfth fairy to put them to sleep too.
The whole castle soon fell into a deep slumber.

A thick hedge of roses grew around the castle until
it was completely hidden from the outside world.

The legend of the Sleeping Beauty spread across the land.

People from all over the world tried to reach the castle to wake her with their kiss, but the vicious rose thorns kept them away.

Until, after one hundred years had
passed, a prince came to the castle.

He rode through the roses,
which seemed to part like
magic before him.

He walked through the sleeping castle, passing servants and dogs resting in the halls, until he came to the chamber where Rose slept.

The prince thought Rose was the most beautiful girl
he'd ever seen. He gently kissed her and she woke up.
They fell in love at first sight.

The curse was lifted and the
castle woke up around them.

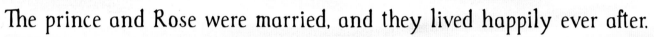

The prince and Rose were married, and they lived happily ever after.

Next Steps

Discussion and comprehension

Ask the children the following questions and discuss their answers.

- Why was the thirteenth fairy so angry?
- How long did Rose go to sleep for?
- Which character do you like best in this story? Why?
- What do you think the world would look like if you woke up after being asleep for 100 years?

Learn letter writing

Ask the children to write a letter to the thirteenth fairy asking her to change her mind about cursing Rose. Ask them to give at least two reasons why she might change her mind. For example, 'Rose and her family are really nice', 'they didn't really mean not to invite you', '100 years is a really long time for Rose to go to sleep'. Write your own letter for the children to use as an example.

Make a hat for a feast

Give the children a range of gold and silver coloured card, paper, shiny stickers and fabric. Staple or glue together a hat for each child, in either a basic crown shape or cone shape. Then ask them to decorate their hat for a royal party. Show them some examples of hats that they could make by looking at the hats guests are wearing at the beginning of the story.